غاسلات اسياب المنوحِشات

THE WILD WASHERWOMEN

John Yeoman   Quentin Blake

MANTRA LINGUA

Arabic translation by Abdul Wahab Al-Tahan

First published in Great Britain 1979 by Hamish Hamilton Ltd
This dual language edition published by arrangement with Anderson Press Ltd, London
Text Copyright © 1979 John Yeoman
Illustration Copyright © 1979 Quentin Blake
The rights of John Yeoman and Quentin Blake to be identified as the author and illustrator of this work
have been asserted by them in accordance with the Copyright, Designs and Patents Act, 1988.

Dual language text copyright © 2012 Mantra Lingua Ltd
Audio copyright © 2012 Mantra Lingua Ltd
This edition first published in 2012 by Mantra Lingua Ltd
Mantra Lingua, Global House, 303 Ballards Lane, London, N12 8NP
www.mantralingua.com

ISBN 978 1 84611 760 2

A CIP record of this book is available from the British Library

في أحد الأيام كان هناك سبعة نساء يعملن في غسيل الثياب.

Once upon a time there were seven washerwomen.

في كل يوم كن يذهبن إلى النهر وعلى رؤوسهن سلال مليئة بالثياب الوسخة.

Every day they went down to the river with their baskets of washing on their heads.

أسمائهن كانت : دوتي، لوتي، مولي، ويني، ميني، ارنستين وكن جميعهن صديقات حميمات.

Their names were Dottie, Lottie, Molly, Dolly, Winnie, Minnie and Ernestine, and they were all good friends.

كن عندما يصلن إلى النهر يفرزن الثياب ويبللنها في الماء ثم يضعن الصابون عليها ويفركنها بالحجارة لتنظيفها.

When they got to the river they
sorted out the clothes and plunged
them in. They soaked them.
They soaped them.
They pounded them
on the stones.

وبعد ذلك يشطفنها في الماء ويعصرنها وينشرنها فوق الصخور والشجيرات حتى تجف.

They rinsed them. They wrung them.
And they spread them over bushes
and rocks to dry.

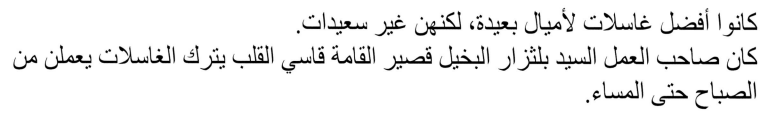

كانوا أفضل غاسلات لأميال بعيدة، لكنهن غير سعيدات.
كان صاحب العمل السيد بلثزار البخيل قصير القامة قاسي القلب يترك الغاسلات يعملن من الصباح حتى المساء.

They were the best washerwomen for miles, but they were not happy.
The owner of the laundry, Mr Balthazar Tight, was a very mean little man, and kept them working from morning to night.

كل صباح عليهن الاستيقاظ منذ الفجر لكوي الغسيل قبل أن يأتِ غسيل اليوم الوسخ .
وكل صباح يأتي صبي يحمل لهم الغسيل ويقول لهن : "أيها السيدات أنا آسف الغسيل اليوم أكثر
من أي وقت مضى".

Every morning at the crack of dawn they had to get up and do the ironing before the day's washing arrived. And every morning the delivery boy, would say, "I'm sorry, ladies, but it's more than ever today."

في صباح أحد الأيام حدق الغاسلات بحزن في جبل الغسيل القذر أمامهن وشعرن أن الغسيل كان أكثر من طاقتهن فتنهدن جميعاً عندما نظرن إلى :

One morning, as the washerwomen stared glumly at the mountain o
dirty laundry, they felt that it was really too much. They all sighed
as they looked at the

الشراشف القذرة
filthy sheets,

المحارم الوسخة
grubby hankies,

الجوارب المقرفة
horrid socks,

قمصان النوم الوسخة
grimy nightshirts,

مفارش الطاولات المبعثرة

messy tablecloths

المناشف المخيفة

and ghastly towels.

"لماذا لا نترك هذا العمل؟" اقترحت ارنستين بخجل.

"Why don't we just leave it?"
suggested Ernestine timidly.

أشرقت وجوههن في الحال!
"لماذا لم نفكر في ذلك من قبل؟" ويني ضاحكة . ثم أخذن بالرقص.
فُتِحَ الباب فجأة ودخل السيد بلثزار البخيل وقال : "الآن، الآن أيها السيدات" وهو عابس،
"يوجد عمل يجب إنهاءه".

Their faces brightened up immediately.
"Why didn't we think of it before?" chortled Winnie.
And at that they began to dance.
The door burst open and
Mr Balthazar Tight stepped in.
"Now, now, ladies,"
he said with a frown.
"There's work to be done."

نظر السيد بلثزار إلى كومة الغسيل الضخمة وقال : "رائع" هناك غسيل أكثر من أي وقت مضى.
صاحت ميني بغضب : "دعونا ننتقم منه يابنات".

Then he looked at the great mound of laundry.
"Wonderful," he said, "there's more than ever."
This made Minnie so angry that she shouted, "Let him have it, girls!"

ثم دفعت الغاسلات السبعة كومة الغسيل القذر فوق رأس بلثزار البخيل فغمرته ثم فروا خارج قاعة الغسيل إلى الفناء.

And the seven washerwomen pushed the mountain of laundry until it collapsed on top of Mr Balthazar Tight. Then they raced out of the laundry and into the yard.

وحشروا أنفسهن في عربة الماعز وأمسكت دوتي زمام
العجلة وصاحت : "هيا".

They piled into the empty goat-cart
and Dottie grabbed the reins.
"Gee up," she cried to the goat.

ومن كثرة فرح الغاسلات بهروبهن دفعوا بالعربة إلى بركة ماء البلدة
فرشموا ثياب المارة النظيفة بالمياه الموحلة.

The washerwomen were so excited by their escape that they drove the cart
right through the town pond, splashing the clean clothes of the passers-by
with muddy water.

بعد ذلك لم يعد هنا شيء يوقفهم واتجهوا إلى السوق
فقلبوا أكشاك البيع وأطلقوا الحيوانات.

After that there was no stopping them. They rode
to the market place, where they overturned
the stalls and set the animals loose.

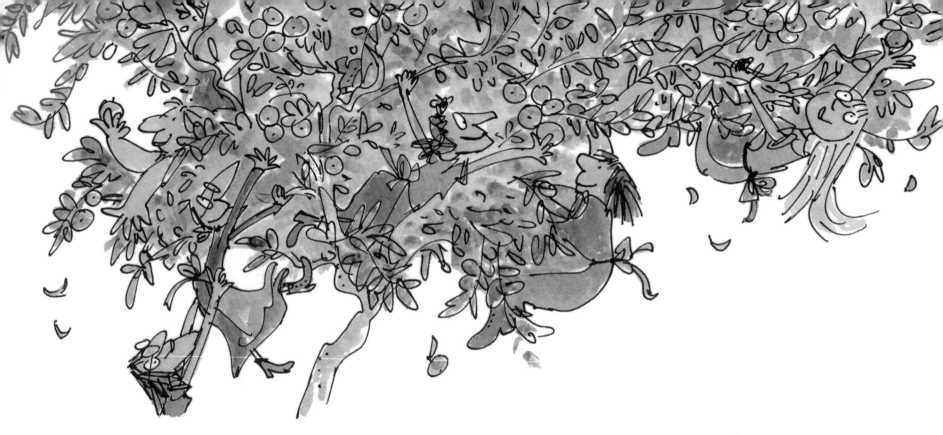

ثم توقفن في البساتين وتسلقن الأشجار وأخذن يقطفن الفاكهة من دون إذن المزارعين. ثم تسابقن إلى دكان بيع القبعات وانتزعنها.

They stopped in orchards and climbed the trees to help themselves to the farmers' fruit.
They raced through the hat shops and snatched the hats.

ثم ركضن إلى الكنائس وتأرجحن على حبال الأجراس وأحدثن ضجيجاً أزعج السكان المحليين.

They ran into churches and alarmed the local people by swinging
on the bell ropes and making a terrible noise.

استمتع الغاسلات بكثير من المرح بحيث لم يرغبن في الإنتهاء منه. العمل في الغسيل المتواصل أكسبهن قوة بحيث لم يستطع الناس منعهن من عمل أي شيء.

The washerwomen were having so much fun that they didn't want it to end. All that washing had made them very strong. The people who tried to stop them didn't have a chance.

كل واحد كان خائف منهن، ولذلك كل قرية بنت برجاً للمراقبة بحيث عندما يرى أحد القرويين
عربة الماعز الخاصة بهن يصرخ : "انظروا الغاسلات المتوحشات قادمات!"

Everyone was terrified of them. Each village built a watch-tower so that a villager
could shout, "Look out, the wild washerwomen are coming!" when their goat-cart
came into sight.

كان يعيش في كوخ في الغابة سبعة حطابين، وعندما سمعوا بأن الغاسلات السبعة قادمات ضحكوا وقالوا : "سوف نرى من سيخاف، وسوف نحضر لهن مفاجأة".

In a hut in the forest lived seven woodcutters. When they heard that the seven washerwomen were coming they just laughed. "We'll see who's afraid," they said. "We'll prepare a surprise for them."

قام الحطابون بنفش شعورهم وعقدوا لحاهم ودهنوا أنفسهم بالطين والأوساخ. ثم دربوا أنفسهم على صرخات مريعة لإخافة الغاسلات.

The woodcutters made themselves as ugly and as frightening as possible. They tangled their hair and matted their beards. They smeared mud and soot over their hands and faces and clothes. And they practised making blood-curdling cries.

قَدِم النسوة السبعة في الحال يتمايلن ويصعدن في الطريق الجبلي بـعربة الماعز
وحين التفوا مع الطريق شاهدوا شيئاً مرعباً.

Soon the seven washerwomen came rattling up the mountain path in
their goat-cart. As they turned a corner, there in front of them was
a terrifying sight.

لكن ميني لاحظت أن ما تراه هو أقذر شيء شاهدنه في أي وقت مضى من حياتهن.
فصاحت: "تعالوا يا بنات" وتذكروا بأنكن غاسلات ثياب.

But then Minnie realised that they were looking at the
dirtiest and grubbiest things that they had ever seen in
their lives. "Come on, girls," she shouted.
"Remember you're washerwomen!"

نزلن من عربة الماعز وأمسكن بالحطابين ووضعوهم في الماء فغسلوهم وفركوهم بالحجارة ثم عصروهم ونشروهم ليجفوا.

They leapt out of the cart and grabbed hold of the woodcutters. They plunged them in the river. They soaked them and squeezed them, and pounded them on the stones. They rinsed them and wrung them and laid them out to dry.

عندما انتهى النسوة من عملهن ظهر الحطابون نظيفين وسيمين كما لم يظهروا من قبل، وشعرت النسوة بالفخر لعملهن. وعندما رأت النسوة الحطابين من دون الأوساخ والطين أحبوا شكلهم وفكرن أنه من الممكن أن يكونوا أزواجاً لهن.

By the time they had finished the woodcutters had never looked so clean, and the washerwomen felt quite proud of their work. In fact, now they could see the woodcutters without their soot and mud, they really rather liked the look of them.

تزوج الحطابون من الغاسلات اللذين بنوا لهن أكواخاً من الخشب ليعشن فيها، وكان الناس الذين يسافرون من خلال الجبل يشاهدون الحطابين والغاسلات سعداء بالغسيل وتقطيع الأشجار ويعيشون أجمل أوقات حياتهم.

The washerwomen married the woodcutters, who built them some new log huts to live in. People who travelled along the mountain path would see them, all happily washing and woodcutting and having the time of their lives.

Other Arabic and English books for 6-10 year olds

Alfie's Angels
Ali Baba and the Forty Thieves
Beowulf
Buri and the Marrow
Children of Lir
Dragon's Tears
Ellie's Secret Diary
Farmer Duck
Fox Fables
Giant Turnip
Goldilocks and the Three Bears
Goose Fables
Grandma's Saturday Soup

Isis and Osiris
Journey Through Islamic Arts
Keeping up with Cheetah
Li's Chinese New Year
Lima's Red Hot Chilli
Lion Fables
Marek and Alice's Christmas
My Bilingual Talking Dictionary
Not Again Red Riding Hood
Pandora's Box
Pied Piper
Samira's Eid
Sports Day in the Jungle
That's My Mama!
The Wibbly Wobbly Tooth
Wild Washerwomen
Yeh Hsien, the Chinese Cinderella
You're All My Favourites